DINOSAUR CLUB

Escaping the Liopleurodon

Written by Rex Stone

Illustrated by Louise Forshaw

Jamie has just moved to Ammonite Bay, a stretch of coastline famed for its fossils. Jamie is a member of the Dinosaur Club—a network of kids who share dinosaur knowledge, help identify fossils, post new discoveries, and talk about all things prehistoric. Jamie carries his tablet everywhere in case he needs to contact the Club.

Jamie is exploring Ammonite Bay when he meets Tess, another member of the Dinosaur Club. Tess takes Jamie to a cave with a strange tunnel and some dinosaur footprints. When they walk along the footprints, the two new friends find themselves back in the time of the dinosaurs!

It's amazing, but dangerous, too—and they'll definitely need help from the Dinosaur Club…

CONTENTS

CHAPTER 1

Hurry up, Tess! Jamie Morgan thought as
a wave lapped around his ankles, swirling
the sand beneath his bare feet.

Jamie was going snorkeling in
Ammonite Bay and his best friend Tess
Clay was late. He scanned the empty
beach, squinting in the sunshine.

Suddenly, he spotted Tess running
across the sand with her snorkel and

mask dangling over one arm, a
bodyboard in the other and her
binoculars around her neck.

'You can't go bodyboarding today,'
Jamie called. 'The ocean's as flat as
a pancake.'

'I'm not going bodyboarding.' Tess
grinned, skidding to a halt. 'In fact I'm
not going in that ocean at all.'

'Not even snorkeling?' asked
Jamie, disappointed.

Tess shook her head.
'Not here.'

'Around the headland
then?' asked Jamie. Tess
had lived in Ammonite
Bay all her life, so she
knew the best places.

'No—much farther away than that.'
Tess's grin was nearly splitting her face.
'But we can be there in an instant.'

'You mean…' Jamie began.

'The Jurassic ocean!' Tess finished.

Jamie and Tess shared a fantastic
secret. They'd found a way to visit a
world of living dinosaurs. The only
people they'd told about it were their
friends in Dinosaur Club, a network of
kids around the world who loved
everything prehistoric.

'Cool!' exclaimed Jamie. He could already feel bubbles of excitement inside him. 'Good thing I never go anywhere without my backpack.'

'And I've still got the Jurassic ammonite,' Tess said, glancing down at her shorts pocket, as the two friends raced toward the cliff path on Smugglers' Point. They knew that the age of the fossil they carried with them determined which time period they visited.

'Cool,' Jamie replied. 'But why do you have a bodyboard when we're going snorkeling?'

'It's for Wanna,' Tess explained as they
neared the rocks that led up to their
secret cave. 'He can ride while we swim.
It's even got one of his prehistoric friends
on it.' She stopped at the top of the cliff
and turned the board over. Printed
underneath it was a fearsome-looking
reptile with four powerful flippers. Its
open mouth showed off sharp, scary-
looking teeth.

Jamie took his tablet out of his backpack, opened the DinoData app, and scanned the picture. 'Liopleurodon,' he read. 'Most successful aquatic hunter in the Jurassic; a type of Plesiosaur.' Jamie stuffed the tablet back into his backpack. 'I don't think a plesiosaur would call Wanna its friend. It would call him dinner.'

Liopleurodon

Jamie and Tess scrambled up the rocks to the old smugglers' cave and the hidden entrance to Dino World. They squeezed into the secret chamber at the back, and Jamie shined his flashlight onto the line of fossilized footprints.

'Ready for action?' said Jamie.

'You bet!' Tess replied.

They put their feet over each clover-shaped print. 'One, two, three, four… five!'

In an instant, Jamie and Tess were walking out among the huge trees of the Jurassic jungle. Giant dragonflies buzzed around them like model airplanes in the steaming air.

'Phew! It's as hot as ever,' said Tess, wiping her forehead. 'Just right for a swim.'

Grunk!

There was a rustling in the spiky horsetail plants nearby, and a little green and brown wannanosaurus burst out.

'Hello, Wanna!' Tess patted their dinosaur friend on his hard-domed head and Wanna wagged his tail in excitement.

Jamie picked some ginkgoes from an overhanging tree. 'Good thing his favorite fruit grows in Cretaceous and Jurassic times.' He tossed two to Wanna and hid the rest in his backpack. Wanna gobbled up the snacks and rushed around on his stumpy legs, giving Jamie and Tess sticky nuzzles.

Jamie took out his notebook with the map he'd drawn of the Jurassic Dino World. 'This says that the sea is southwest from the cave. Got your compass?'

'Of course.' Tess pulled it out of her pocket and pointed to the southwest. 'Through the trees here.' The three friends set off over the hills, walking through the conifers and deep ferns until they arrived on the edge of a cliff, looking out over the beautiful ocean. To their right was a calm, sparkling bay shielded from the waves by a line of jet black rocks poking up out of the water.

'Awesome!' exclaimed Tess. 'With those rocks as barriers, that bay's just like a swimming pool.'

'The perfect place for snorkeling,' said Jamie. 'And we can climb down that pathway where the cliff's crumbled away.'

'Last one to the beach is a sea slug!' yelled Tess.

CHAPTER 2

'Beat you!' Jamie laughed as he clambered over the last of the slippery black slate rocks onto the sand.

'Only just,' said Tess, sliding down beside him. 'Anyway, Wanna's the sea slug.'

Wanna scampered happily up behind.

'Do you think he remembers our last trip to the seaside?' asked Jamie. 'He had quite an adventure with his flying reptile friends.'

Tess grinned. 'Who knows what goes on inside that domed head?'

As they headed along the sand,
Tess pointed to the biggest rock out
in the bay. 'It looks like the back of a
sea monster with a fin sticking up
in the middle.'

'We'll call it Fin Rock,' Jamie
decided. The tall rock stood like
a gate to the open sea and
waves splashed up against
it on the ocean side.

Beyond the line of rocks, Jamie could
see something on the surface of
the ocean. 'Wow!'

Tess saw it too and looked through
her binoculars. 'There's more than one!'
She thrust the binoculars at Jamie.

Through them, he saw several
creatures moving through the waves.
Their long, pointed noses made them
look like prehistoric dolphins.

Jamie passed the binoculars back to Tess, took his tablet out of his backpack, and snapped a photo of the creatures. 'Back in the Jurassic,' he typed. 'Anyone know what these are?' He sent the message to their Dinosaur Club friends.

The screen flashed with replies from around the world. Tess peered over Jamie's shoulder to read them too.

'Ichthyosaurs,' wrote Nora from Canada. 'They look so cool!'

 'They ate fish and squid,' added Lethabo, who was from South Africa.

'Their eyes are really big,' replied Kim from Vietnam. 'So they had good eyesight to help them hunt their food.'

'Thanks guys!' typed Jamie. He stowed the tablet away again.

'Those ichthyosaurs look like they're having fun,' Tess said. 'We should, too. Let's go snorkeling!'

They were both already wearing their swimsuits underneath their clothes, so in a few moments they were ready. They left their clothes, shoes, and the backpack on a dry rock, grabbed their masks and snorkels, and waded into the warm shallows. Tess carried the bodyboard.

The water was so clear that Jamie could see his toes and the pebbles on the sand.

Wanna dashed after them, but skidded to a halt at the sight of the tiny waves.

'Don't worry!' Tess laughed. 'They won't hurt you.'

'I know what'll get him in.' Jamie ran back onto the beach to his backpack and pulled out a ginkgo fruit.

He backed slowly into the water keeping it just out of Wanna's reach. The little dinosaur followed eagerly, but when the water lapped over his feet, he darted away again.

Jamie pretended to take a big bite out of the stinky ginkgo. 'Yum, yum!'

Wanna took a few steps forward,

wading up to his knees in the water.

'That's it, boy,' Jamie said. 'Come and get your tasty snack.' He put the ginkgo on the bodyboard as Tess held it still.

Grunk!

Wanna scrambled on to the bodyboard making it wobble in the water. Jamie held Wanna's waist as the little dinosaur got his balance.

'He looks like a surfer now,' chuckled Tess, letting go of the board.

'Champion of the waves,' said Jamie
But when Wanna bent down to eat his
ginkgo, he overbalanced and
somersaulted into the ocean. He sat in
the shallow water looking very surprised.

'Poor old Wanna,' said Jamie, trying
not to laugh. He and Tess helped him on
again. This time Wanna managed to stay
afloat, but looked mournfully at the
ginkgo which was floating away. Jamie
grabbed it and Wanna ate it gratefully.

'I think you've earned that,' said Tess.

Jamie put his hand firmly through the loop of the bodyboard's rope. 'Stay still and I'll pull you along,' he said to Wanna.

'Masks on!' declared Tess.

They pulled their masks over their faces.

'Check!' said Jamie.

'Snorkels in.'

Jamie placed the snorkel in his mouth and gave an excited thumbs up.

They waded out until the water came up to their armpits and then started swimming. They put their faces in the water so that their snorkels pointed up into the air. Jamie looked down,

breathing through his snorkel. Below him, small plants waved in the gentle current and weird, colorful sea creatures darted up and down. An electric blue sea slug crept over a rock. Then a group of squid-like creatures came swimming by. Their spiral shells were wonderful colors—blues, greens, and purples.

And there were real-live ammonites that were so bright. The ammonites were nothing like the brown and gray fossils he and Tess often dug up back at home.

Jamie could see Tess was having fun, too. He made an O shape with his thumb and forefinger, the "okay" sign for divers. Tess signed back and made a face like a blubbery fish. Jamie burst out laughing and they both came up, gasping for air.

Wanna grunked cheerfully at them. He was obviously enjoying himself as much as they were.

Jamie and Tess looked down again. A shoal of large cuttlefish drifted past.

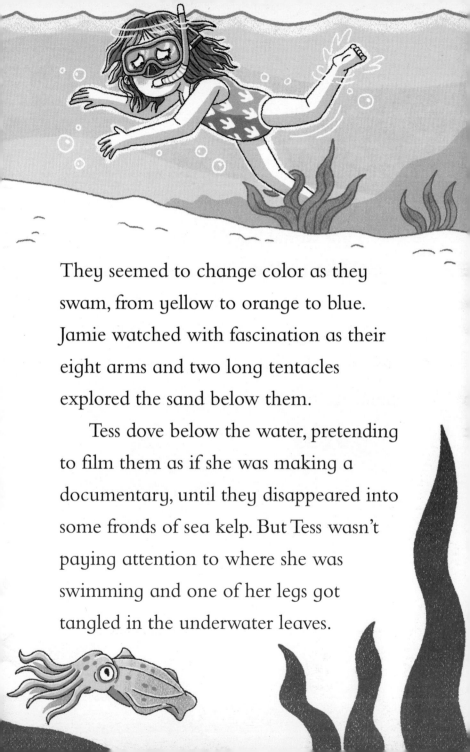

They seemed to change color as they
swam, from yellow to orange to blue.
Jamie watched with fascination as their
eight arms and two long tentacles
explored the sand below them.

Tess dove below the water, pretending
to film them as if she was making a
documentary, until they disappeared into
some fronds of sea kelp. But Tess wasn't
paying attention to where she was
swimming and one of her legs got
tangled in the underwater leaves.

As quick as he could, Jamie dove down into the tangle to pull his friend free.

'Thanks, Jamie,' Tess said as they surfaced.

'That would have made a good TV show,' Jamie joked, adjusting his mask on his face. 'Attack of the Killer Kelp!'

Tess laughed, but stopped suddenly. 'Wait—where's the bodyboard?'

Jamie glanced down at his wrist. The rope was gone! 'It must have slipped off.' They looked around frantically for their little dino friend.

'Over there,' said Tess, pointing.

Wanna was sitting happily on his board, peering down into the water, completely unaware that he was drifting toward the deep, dangerous ocean beyond Fin Rock.

'Wanna!' yelled Jamie in alarm.

They swam quickly through the water after their friend, breathing through their snorkels so that they could swim as fast as possible. Jamie could see the seabed sloping away beneath him and the water getting deeper and deeper.

He pulled hard with his arms and kicked furiously. Glancing up through his splashes, he could see that they were nearing the wide gap in the rock barrier, and the rough, foaming water beyond. Wanna was going to be swept out to sea! Jamie wasn't going to let that happen.

Suddenly, Jamie was close enough to see the bright yellow rope ahead of him. He tried to grab it but it slipped through his fingers. Wanna and the bodyboard had reached the gap next to Fin Rock and were bobbing on the choppy water at the edge of the shallow bay. Beyond was the ocean, so deep and dark that Jamie couldn't see the bottom.

He kicked forward again and grabbed the loop of the rope, holding on with all his strength as the board tugged against him in the rough water.

'Got him!' he yelled to Tess, his snorkel banging against his cheek.

'Just in time,' Tess said as she swam up. 'Let's get away from here.'

Jamie could feel the board wobbling violently in the waves. Wanna gave a frightened grunk.

'Don't worry, boy,' Jamie told him. 'You'll be safe soon.'

But the little dinosaur didn't seem to understand. He kicked his feet and waved his tail wildly, eyes wide with fear.

'No, Wanna!' shouted Tess. 'Stop!'

The board rocked more and more violently until…

SPLASH!

Wanna disappeared under the water.

CHAPTER 3

Jamie dropped the rope, took a deep
breath, and dove. He caught hold of
Wanna's flailing front leg and kicked for
the surface. Wanna emerged spluttering,
then went under again. Jamie had taken
lifeguard classes, but they hadn't gone
over how to rescue a dinosaur! He swam
around behind Wanna, avoiding the
flapping feet, and grasped him around
his neck, pulling him to the surface.

Jamie had to kick hard to stay afloat as Wanna struggled in panic.

'Keep still, boy!' he spluttered, as he swam to the edge of Fin Rock. When Jamie finally reached the rock, Tess helped give Wanna a shove to get the little dinosaur up onto the flat part of Fin Rock. Jamie stayed in the water, clinging to the rock, to get his breath back.

Safely on the rock, Wanna sneezed
and then spotted some seaweed.

Grunk!

He started eating
the slimy leaves as if
nothing had happened. Jamie smiled
and hauled himself out. He pulled his
mask down around his neck, like Tess
had done.

'Looks like we've lost the bodyboard,'
Tess said, indicating out to see where the
board floated away with the waves. 'And
if scientists discover a bodyboard next to
a dinosaur fossil, we could mess up all of
history. Not to mention that we're going
to have a hard time getting Wanna back
to the beach.'

Jamie groaned. 'I'm sorry. It's all my fault. I dropped the rope.'

'You were saving me from killer kelp at the time.' Tess grinned. 'Anyway, it was my stupid idea to bring Wanna snorkeling with us.'

Jamie watched the bodyboard being tossed around by the ocean as he tried to think of how to get Wanna back to shore, when suddenly, a sleek, blue-gray creature appeared on the surface, before diving smoothly back into the water.

'An ichthyosaur,' breathed Tess. 'That's awesome!'

'Two of them,' Jamie said as another ichthyosaur knocked the bodyboard with its nose.

'Three!' yelled Tess in excitement as one more head popped out of the choppy water. It caught the board between its teeth and swam away.

'I think they're bringing it back,' said Tess.

The ichthyosaurs swam right up to Fin Rock. One of them nudged the bodyboard toward Jamie and Tess.

Tess and Jamie bent down to get a close look at the sleek marine reptile eyeing them from the water.

'It's smaller than the other two,' said Jamie. 'I reckon it's a young one, but it's still as big as a dolphin.'

'It has a dolphin's snout,' agreed Tess. 'Only it's longer and thinner—and it has an extra set of flippers.'

'And plenty of teeth,' Jamie replied,
'but while they look similar to dolphins,
ichthyosaurs are reptiles, not mammals.'
The ichthyosaur let go of the bodyboard
and it banged against the rock.

'Thanks!' Tess laughed. 'We'll be more
careful next time.' She fished the board
out of the water.

Grunk! Wanna agreed.

The ichthyosaur turned away and
swam off into the shallow water of the
bay. The others plunged after it.

Tess slid the bodyboard down
onto the calm water on the bay side
of the rock.
'Better get Wanna back to dry land.'

Jamie put his mask on, his snorkel
back in, and then jumped into the sea.

'Come on, boy,' he coaxed, patting
the board.

Grunk! Wanna sounded anxious. He
began to stamp his feet.

'You'll be all right, I promise,' said
Tess. 'We'll keep the board steady.'

Grunk, grunk, GRUNK!

Wanna was jumping up and down
now, drumming his tail on the rock. His
eyes were fixed on the ocean.

'What's wrong?' asked Jamie.

'He's frightened,' said Tess. 'And so are the ichthyosaurs.' In the bay the creatures were now circling anxiously, making an urgent, clamoring whistle.

Jamie pulled his mask on and ducked under the surface.

From the depths of the ocean, a huge, dark shape was swimming up through the water, heading for the bay. It had a long, crocodile-like head and four strong flippers on its massive body. It was the real-life monster on the bodyboard—a Liopleurodon, the deadliest creature in the ocean.

And it was coming straight for him!

CHAPTER 4

'Liopleurodon,' spluttered Jamie. 'I've got to get out!'

Tess didn't waste a second. She hauled her friend onto the rock and pulled the board up after him.

'Thanks,' panted Jamie, pulling down his mask. 'That sea monster's huge.' They turned to see the Liopleurodon break the surface of the water. It was at least five times as long as one of the ichthyosaurs.

Its massive jaws stretched like a grin, showing conical teeth that glistened in the sun.

Jamie and Tess watched in horror as the Liopleurodon swam straight past Fin Rock and into the bay.

'It's after the ichthyosaurs,' said Tess.

The ichthyosaurs waited in the bay, watching the huge creature approach.

Suddenly, with a flick of their tails, they shot toward the gap in the rocks trying to escape into the deep ocean. But the Liopleurodon was too big for the ichthyosaurs to get around.

'They're trapped!' said Jamie.

The Liopleurodon kept its enormous body blocking their escape route to the ocean, and each time the ichthyosaurs tried to make for the open sea, the monster snapped with its fearsome teeth. The water churned like a whirlpool as the creatures struggled.

'The little one's getting tired,' said Tess.

'And that nasty Liopleurodon knows it,' added Jamie grimly.

The little ichthyosaur made another dash for it, but the sea monster plunged down under the water with a huge splash. Jamie and Tess held their breath. When the Liopleurodon's head rose again they could see the young ichthyosaur thrashing helplessly in its jaws. Its friends called to it anxiously.

"Oh no!" Jamie felt horrible watching the frantic ichthyosaur.

The Liopleurodon shook its prize in triumph. But one of the ichthyosaurs dived and swam at the monster, attacking the soft underside of its belly, making the Liopleurodon let go of its prey. The little ichthyosaur darted away.

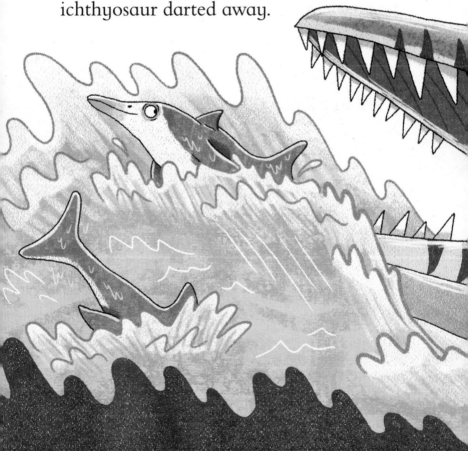

'One zero to the ichthyosaurs!' yelled
Tess, almost falling off the rock in delight.

'They haven't won yet,' Jamie
reminded him. 'They're still trapped.'

'They helped us,' said Tess
determinedly. 'We have to help them.'

'You're right,' agreed Jamie.
'But how?'

Tess quickly scanned their craggy island and went over to a spur of rock with a deep crack in it. She slid her fingers in and heaved.

'This is no time for weightlifting,' said Jamie.

'I'm not weightlifting,' puffed Tess, red in the face with the effort. 'This rock is loose. We can… throw it… at the Liopleurodon. That might scare it off.'

Jamie helped. Soon the rock came away. The friends picked it up between them and staggered to the water's edge.

'We'll give that creature something to think about!' shouted Tess.

'One, two, three, HEAVE!'

They lobbed the rock as hard as they could. It fell with a great splash near the monster. But the Liopleurodon barely flinched.

It plowed on through the water after its prey. Its thick tail slapped down, splashing another huge wave over Fin Rock. Jamie and Tess clung on, digging fingers and toes into any hold in the rock they could find. Wanna clung to them and grunked anxiously.

'That was close,' gasped Tess.

'Quick!' yelled Jamie.

'The bodyboard.'

The board was floating away into the bay. Tess grabbed the bodyboard's rope just in time.

'Good save,' said Jamie.

Tess was just putting the loop around her wrist to make it secure when Jamie noticed that they were in trouble. 'Quick!' Jamie shouted. 'The monster's seen it.'

'Wait,' Tess said. 'I've got an idea.'

Jamie saw the Liopleurodon's beady eyes just above the surface of the water. They were staring at the bobbing board. 'That monster will break it to pieces,' Jamie said.

'Hold on,' Tess replied. She gave
the rope a shake, making the bodyboard
shudder. The Liopleurodon glided toward
it like a deadly crocodile after its prey, its
jaws opening wide. Suddenly it lunged,
but Tess quickly flicked the board up and
onto the rock and the Liopleurodon
missed entirely.

Jamie gave a whoop of delight. 'Go, Tess!' he called. 'It's forgotten all about the ichthyosaurs.'

Tess threw the board out again. Again the Liopleurodon lunged and Tess jerked it away.

Jamie looked at the ichthyosaurs' progress and saw that they had made it to the gap in the rocks. 'They're escaping!' Jamie cried, but then Tess slipped down the wet rock. From the ground, she couldn't throw the board out again.

'You do it!' Tess said, throwing the rope up to Jamie.

Jamie grabbed the rope, knowing he needed to keep the monster busy until the ichthyosaurs were safely away. He flung the bodyboard out like Tess had done— but this time the Liopleurodon was ready. As soon as it saw the bright board slapping down onto the water it grabbed it in its teeth and pulled hard. Jamie didn't have a chance to let go of the rope.

He was catapulted off the rock and into the water!

CHAPTER 5

The water roared in Jamie's ears as he was dragged along the surface by the sea monster into the bay. White foam swirled around him, and he wished he had had his mask on.

Suddenly the pulling stopped. Jamie looked ahead and could just make out through the water that the Liopleurodon had turned. It floated on the water, its

beady eyes just above the surface. They
were looking straight at him.

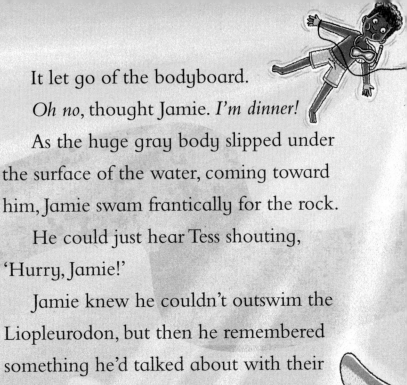

It let go of the bodyboard.

Oh no, thought Jamie. *I'm dinner!*

As the huge gray body slipped under
the surface of the water, coming toward
him, Jamie swam frantically for the rock.

He could just hear Tess shouting,
'Hurry, Jamie!'

Jamie knew he couldn't outswim the
Liopleurodon, but then he remembered
something he'd talked about with their

Dinosaur Club friends—that some predators lost interest when their prey stopped moving. He had nothing to lose. Jamie took a huge breath and stopped swimming. He quickly made a star with his arms and legs and lay there, floating face-down in the water.

He watched, his heart pounding hard, as the Liopleurodon swam in circle below, watching him.

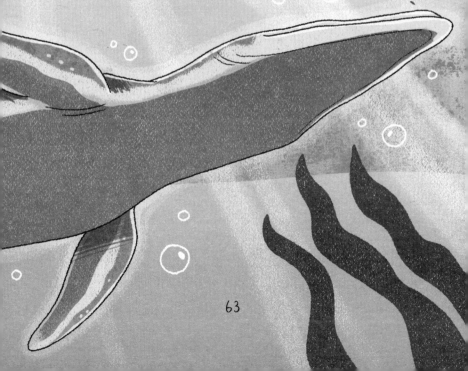

Jamie knew he couldn't move a muscle. The bodyboard rope was still tied around his wrist, tugging at him. He had to fight to keep his arm still, but his plan was working! The sea monster wasn't attacking anymore. It had lost interest. But he knew that as soon as he lifted his head for air it could be back on to him like a shot.

Please go! he thought, desperately willing the sea monster to swim away. But it didn't. Jamie felt like his lungs were going to burst.

Suddenly he heard a great barrage of activity in the water. Something was coming from the deep ocean. The Liopleurodon had heard it, too. It whipped around to see what it was. Jamie took his chance. He lifted his head and gulped in air.

Then he saw a wonderful sight.
Several sleek, gray ichthyosaurs were
speeding toward the bay. Jamie could
see their three little ichthyosaur friends
leading the charge!

They made straight for the
Liopleurodon. It thrashed around trying
to ward off the furious attack.

Jamie struck out for the rock and with
Tess's help scrambled out of the water.
Wanna grabbed the bodyboard in his
teeth and pulled it onto the rock.

'Go ichthyosaurs!' yelled Tess.
'You can beat that monster.'

The Liopleurodon reared and plunged, thrashing out angrily to shake off the whirling mass of ichthyosaurs. But there were too many for it.

Jamie, Tess, and Wanna watched as the beast swished its massive tail, sending a final huge wave breaking over Fin Rock, then fled for the open sea.

Jamie and Tess leapt up and down in delight while Wanna grunked eagerly. The sea monster had been beaten!

CHAPTER 6

'That was awesome!' breathed Jamie.

'Those ichthyosaurs saved your life.'
Tess grinned.

Jamie nodded. 'That's right! They
fought off the fiercest creature in the
Jurassic ocean!'

'And they look really happy about it,'
said Tess, pointing.

The group of ichthyosaurs was
swimming all around Fin Rock, their

sleek bodies arcing in and out of the waves. Wanna grunked happily at them.

'Thanks!' Jamie shouted. 'You were great.' He turned to Tess. 'It's a shame we don't know ichthyosaur language.'

'Let's get back to dry land,' said Jamie, putting his mask back on. 'Hop on board, Wanna. The water's safe now.'

Grunk! Wanna looked at the bodyboard that was punctured with large Liopleurodon teeth holes.

'Don't worry, boy,' Tess assured him. 'It's still seaworthy.'

Jamie slid into the water, pulling the bodyboard behind him. Tess held it steady and Wanna wobbled on board.

Holding one side each, Jamie and Tess kicked off for shore.

'I can hear something behind us,' Tess shouted suddenly.

Jamie spun around, spluttering as his mouth filled with water. Then he burst out laughing. 'We've got an escort.'

It was the three young ichthyosaurs swimming along behind them.

Soon Jamie and Tess were close enough to the shore to stand in the waist-deep water.

The smallest ichthyosaur swam around their legs before speeding back to the group and heading for the open sea.

'Thanks again,' called Jamie after them, pulling off his mask entirely.

Grunk!

Wanna jumped off the bodyboard and splashed the last few steps to the beach.

Jamie and Tess picked up the backpack, their clothes, and shoes and made their way back to the cave. Jamie pointed to the huge teeth marks in Tess's board. 'How are we going to explain this?'

'We'll have to pretend it got attacked by a shark,' said Tess with a grin. 'We can only tell the Dinosaur Club what really happened.'

Wanna gave the bodyboard a sniff. Then he trotted off toward the cave. When they got close, Wanna began to gather leaves and twigs in his teeth.

'He's making himself a nest,' said Tess.

'Let's help,' said Jamie, grabbing a handful of ferns. They got to work, gathering sticks and ferns.

Wanna laid a few twigs down, then nudged them here and there, but when Jamie went to put some branches into the structure Wanna grunked loudly.

'I think he's saying they're the wrong way around.' Tess laughed.

Jamie flipped the branches over. 'Is that better?'

Grunk, grunk!

Wanna wagged his tail. Soon he was curled up in his Jurassic nest.

'Sleep tight, boy,' said Tess. They knew that Wanna could return to his home in the Cretaceous period anytime he wanted, so they said goodbye to their faithful friend and stepped backward in the footprints.

As they emerged into the bright sunlight of Ammonite Bay they were surprised to see a crowd of people gathered on the shoreline below.

'What's going on?' Tess asked.

'There's Granddad,' said Jamie. 'Let's find out.'

They scrambled down to the beach
as fast as they could to join
Commander Morgan.

Everyone was staring and pointing
out to sea. Tess made sure she kept the
bodyboard behind her so no one would
notice the teeth marks.

'I was wondering where you two had gone,' Commander Morgan called when he spotted them. 'You've been missing all the fun.'

'What's going on, Granddad?' asked Jamie.

Commander Morgan nodded out toward the bay. As Jamie and Tess watched, the enormous body of a sleek gray creature broke the surface of the water. A tall spout of water shot into the air. The crowd clapped and cheered.

'You don't see many whales in these parts.' Commander Morgan beamed.

'Looks like Ammonite Bay has got its own sea monster,' Jamie whispered to Tess with a wink.

'But it's not as scary as the one back
in Dino World,' Tess whispered back.
'I definitely prefer this one,' Jamie said.

Dinosaur timeline

The Triassic
(250-200 million years ago)

The first period of the Mesozoic Era was the Triassic. During the Triassic, there were very few plants, and the Earth was hot and dry, like a desert. Most of the dinosaurs that lived during the Triassic were small.

The Jurassic
(200-145 million years ago)

The second period of the Mesozoic Era was the Jurassic. During the Jurassic, the Earth became cooler and wetter, which caused many of plants to grow. This created lots of food for dinosaurs that helped them grow big and thrive.

The Cretaceous
(145-66 million years ago)

The third and final period of the Mesozoic Era was the Cretaceous. During the Cretaceous, dinosaurs were at their peak and dominated the Earth, but at the end most of them suddenly became extinct.

Dinosaurs existed during a time on Earth known as the Mesozoic Era. It lasted for more than 180 million years, and was split into three different periods: the Triassic, Jurassic, and the Cretaceous.

Notable dinosaurs from the Triassic

Plateosaurus

Coelophysis

Eoraptor

Notable dinosaurs from the Jurassic

Stegosaurus

Allosaurus

Archaeopteryx

Diplodocus

Notable dinosaurs from the Cretaceous

T. rex

Triceratops

Velociraptor

Iguanodon

MISTY
MOUNTAINS

GINKGO
CANYON

THICK
JUNGLE

DISCOVERY
HILLS

DINO DATA

This predator looked like an enormous crocodile, with four huge flippers that helped it swim speedily through the water. Its size, powerful jaws, and sharp teeth made it the fiercest marine reptile of all time.

Super-smelling nostrils

Name: Liopleurodon

Pronunciation: LIE-oh-PLOOR-oh-don

Period: Jurassic

Size: 23ft (7m) long

Habitat: Oceans and seas

Diet: Marine animals

FACT

Like all marine reptiles, liopleurodon came up to the surface of the water to breathe.

Streamlined body

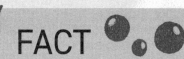

FACT

Liopleurodon was an apex predator, which means it was at the top of its food chain and not hunted by any other animals.

DINO DATA

Ichthyosaurs were a group of marine reptiles that evolved from lizard-like creatures who lived on land, to dolphin-like creatures who lived in water. The most well-known ichthyosaur was called ichthyosaurus.

Paddles for speed

Flippers for balance

Name: Ichthyosaurus
Pronunciation: ICK-thee-oh-sore-us
Period: Triassic to Cretaceous
Size: 10ft (3m) long
Habitat: Oceans and seas
Diet: Fish and other marine animals

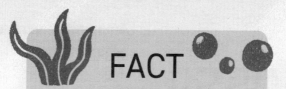

FACT

The name ichthyosaur
means "fish lizard."

Large eyes for good
vision underwater

FACT

Some ichthyosaurs grew new fingers
and finger bones to make their paddles
bigger, so they could swim better.

FOSSIL FACTS

Ammonites were a group of marine animals related to octopuses and squid. They lived in shells that were often beautifully coiled and covered in small ridges.

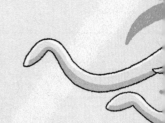

Name: Ammonite

Pronunciation: A-moh-nite

Period: Jurassic to Cretaceous

Size: (½ in (1cm) – 6½ ft 2m) long

Habitat: Oceans and seas

Diet: Plankton, crustaceans, and fish

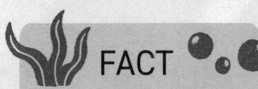

FACT

Ammonites lived their entire lives inside their shells, similar to snails.

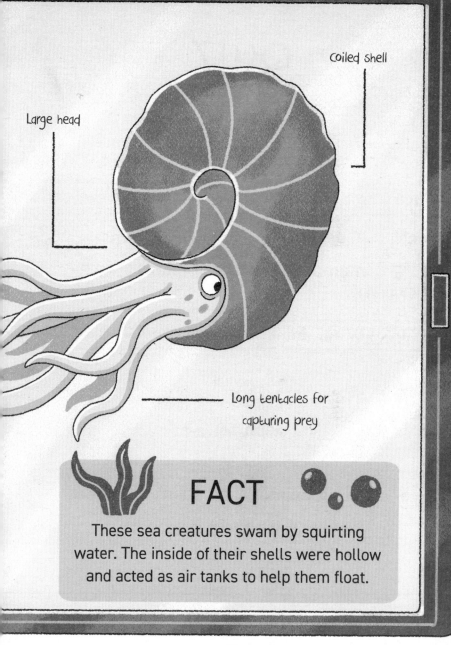

Coiled shell

Large head

Long tentacles for capturing prey

FACT

These sea creatures swam by squirting water. The inside of their shells were hollow and acted as air tanks to help them float.

QUIZ

1   What is the name of the big rock
    the kids discover?

2   True or false: ichthyosaurs were
    mammals, just like dolphins.

3   What did ichthyosaurs eat?

4   True or false: Wanna is an
    excellent swimmer.

5   What animal did the kids encounter
    back in the present day?

6   True or false: Liopleurodon is a
    meat-eater.

CHECK YOUR ANSWERS on page 95

GLOSSARY

AMMONITE
A type of sea creature that lived during the time of the dinosaurs

CARNIVORE
An animal that only eats meat

DINOSAUR
A group of ancient reptiles that lived millions of years ago

FOSSIL
Remains of a living thing that have become preserved over time

GINKGO
A type of tree that dates back millions of years

HERBIVORE
An animal that only eats plant matter

JURASSIC
The second period of the time dinosaurs existed (200-145 million years ago)

PALEONTOLOGIST
A scientist who studies dinosaurs and other fossils

PTEROSAUR
Ancient flying reptiles that existed at the same time as dinosaurs

PREDATOR
An animal that hunts other animals for food

QUIZ ANSWERS
1. Fin Rock
2. False
3. Fish and squid
4. False
5. A whale
6. True

Text for DK by Working Partners Ltd
9 Kingsway, London WC2B 6XF
With special thanks to Jan Burchett and Sara Vogler

Design by Collaborate Ltd
Illustrator Louise Forshaw
Consultant Dougal Dixon

Acquisitions Editor James Mitchem
US Senior Editor Shannon Beatty
Senior Designer and Jacket Designer Elle Ward
Jacket Coordinator Magda Pszuk
Production Editor Abi Maxwell
Senior Production Controller Inderjit Bhullar
Publishing Director Sarah Larter

First American Edition, 2023
Published in the United States by DK Publishing
1745 Broadway, 20th Floor, New York, New York 10019

A catalog record for this book is available from the Library of Congress.

ISBN: 978-0-7440-8026-1 (paperback)
ISBN: 978-0-7440-8027-8 (hardcover)

DK books are available at special discounts when purchased in bulk
for sales promotions, premiums, fund-raising, or educational use.
For details, contact DK Publishing Special Markets, 1745 Broadway,
20th Floor, New York, NY 10019
SpecialSales@dk.com

Printed and bound in Great Britain by
Clays Ltd, Elcograf S.p.A.

www.dk.com
For the curious

MIX
Paper | Supporting
responsible forestry
FSC™ C018179

This book was made with Forest
Stewardship Council™ certified
paper – one small step in DK's
commitment to a sustainable future.
For more information go to
www.dk.com/our-green-pledge